Glow in the Dark Spooky House

Written by Joanne Barkan
Illustrated by Rose Mary Berlin

A GOLDEN BOOK • NEW YORK

Western Publishing Company, Inc., Racine, Wisconsin 53404

(See back cover for special Glow in the Dark directions!)

"Look at that amazing house!" Betsy said.

"That's where Aunt Sarah lives," Betsy's father explained. "Isn't it a wonderful place?"

"No!" Boo said. "It doesn't look wonderful to me. It looks spooky. It looks very spooky all around here!"

Boo was Betsy's younger brother. His real name was John Peter, but everyone called him Boo because he was still afraid of many things. He was afraid of dark rooms, ghosts, monsters, and strange old houses.

"Boo," said his mother, "there's nothing to be afraid of. We're spending a week here in the country with Aunt Sarah. You'll get used to her house and everything around it."

"Welcome!" Aunt Sarah said at the doorway. "It's so nice to see all of you. Betsy, you've grown so tall. And how are you, Boo?"

Boo didn't say anything. He just looked around as he entered the house.

"Boo thinks you have monsters and ghosts in your house," Betsy explained.

Aunt Sarah laughed. "Dear me, no!" she said. "I'm all alone here—except for Shadow, my black cat."

After a snack of milk and cherry pie, Betsy and Boo got ready for bed. They were sleeping in the guest bedroom on the second floor.

"Isn't this a funny old room, Boo?" Betsy asked. "Boo?" she asked again. "Boo! *What* are you doing?"

"I'm checking the closet for ghosts," Boo said.

"There's no such thing," Betsy insisted. "I promise. Let's turn out the lights and go to sleep."

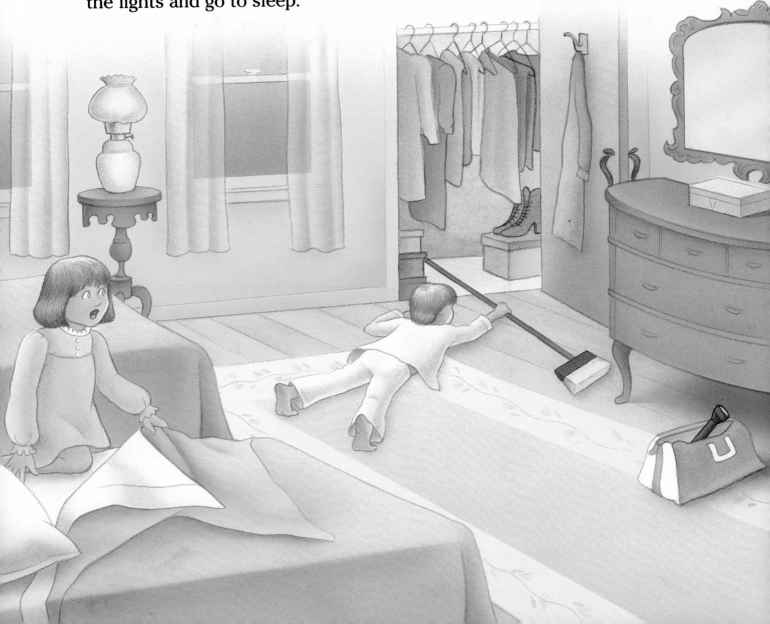

Boo climbed into bed. But before he turned off the lamp, he tucked his flashlight under his pillow. Boo could not fall asleep without his flashlight.

As Betsy and Boo drifted off to sleep the moon rose. Its silver glow shimmered through the curtains. The light spread across the floor and was reflected in the heavy old bedroom mirror, which cast strange shadows on the wall. Then, suddenly, there was a noise in the hallway.

Boo sat straight up in bed. "What was that?" he whispered.
"It might be a horrible monster. A monster outside of our room!"
Boo saw the strange shadows on the wall. He saw the flickering
light. "Oh, no," he gasped. "It's a monster *inside* our room!" There
was no time to reach for the flashlight. There was only time to
scream, "Betsy! Help!"

Betsy awoke with a start. She switched on the lamp. "What's wrong?" she asked. She didn't see anything strange.

"I guess I made a mistake," Boo mumbled as he looked around the room.

But just then the children heard noises overhead.

Creak. Scrape. Tap-tap. C r e a k.   S c r a p e.

Boo leapt out of bed. "I've had enough of this house!" he declared. "I'm going to find Mom and Dad."

Using his flashlight, Boo made his way down the long dark hall. Betsy hurried after her brother.

"This is their room," Boo whispered. He stood in front of the door. It was open just a crack.

Betsy knocked, but there was no answer. She knocked again. When there was still no answer, she took a deep breath and pushed the door open.

Betsy and Boo stepped inside the room. It was empty.
Their parents were gone…but the noises weren't!
Hoo! Hoo! Hoo! they heard.

"A ghost!" Boo screeched with fright.

"No, look!" Betsy said, pointing to the window.

Staring right at them through the glass was a large white owl. Its eyes were gleaming circles of light. But as the owl lifted its wings and flew away, the children heard more sounds overhead.

Creak. Scrape. Tap-tap.

"Come on. Let's find out what that is," said Betsy.

"Not me!" Boo said. But Betsy had already taken the flashlight and was walking toward a steep staircase.

"I can't stay here without my flashlight!" Boo said.

He ran after his sister. Together the children climbed the staircase. Each time they put their feet on a step, it creaked and groaned. As they climbed, they stared at the closed door at the top of the stairs.

"There could be a hundred monsters up there," Boo whispered.

Step. Creak. Groan.

"There could be a thousand ghosts!" Boo whispered.

Step. Creak. Groan. Step. Creak. Groan.

Finally they were standing in front of the door. Betsy reached out and turned the knob. The door opened and—

B O N G...B O N G...B O N G...

Boo grabbed his sister's arm. "What's that noise?"

Betsy shined the flashlight into a large room. It was filled with old furniture, ladders, piles of boxes, and in one corner, a tall grandfather clock. The clock *bonged* ten times.

"Aunt Sarah told me about that clock," Betsy said. "It's over one hundred years old, and she winds it every week."

Boo took one small step into the room to see the old clock. But when he put his foot down, something moved underneath it. Then that something sprang high into the air. It shrieked—a long piercing shriek. Both children screamed, "HELP!"

Betsy and Boo heard quick footsteps. A door at the far end of the room opened. The lights went on.

"Betsy! Boo! Are you all right?"

It was their mother, father, and Aunt Sarah.

"A monster attacked us!" Boo shouted. "It jumped at us. And there are ghosts everywhere. We heard them creaking and groaning and tapping all over the house!"

"Dear me," Aunt Sarah said. "I think your monster was my Shadow." Aunt Sarah held a small black cat in her arms. It looked even more frightened than Boo did.

"The creaking, groaning, and tapping was just all of us walking around this old house," Boo's father said.

"This spooky old house," Boo sniffled.

"But there are wonderful surprises," Boo's mother said, "inside the house and outside, too. Come on. We can show you one right now."

Betsy and Boo followed the three grown-ups. The door at the end of the large room led onto a balcony.

"Look," their mother said, pointing up at the sky.

The children could hardly believe what they saw.

"There must be a million stars!" Betsy said.

"But that's not all," her father added. "Look down there." He pointed to the lawn in front of the house. Six deer stood nibbling in the grass. Their soft white tails glowed in the starlight.

"No monsters anywhere. No ghosts," Aunt Sarah said. "Just twinkling stars and nibbling deer. Aunt Sarah's house isn't so spooky, is it, Boo?"

Boo didn't say anything. Instead he climbed onto Aunt Sarah's lap along with Shadow. Boo watched the deer for a while. Then he watched the twinkling stars.

"No monsters. No ghosts," he murmured.

Boo wrapped his arms around Shadow. Soon he was fast asleep. And he didn't even need his flashlight.